T0193259

TORNADO INTERCEPT

RICHARD MCKENDRICK

WESTBOW
PRESS®
A DIVISION OF THOMAS NELSON
& ZONDERVAN

WestBow Press books may be ordered through booksellers or by contacting:

WestBow Press
A Division of Thomas Nelson & Zondervan
1663 Liberty Drive
Bloomington, IN 47403
www.westbowpress.com
844-714-3454

ISBN: 978-1-6642-7568-3 (sc)
ISBN: 978-1-6642-7569-0 (e)

Library of Congress Control Number: 2022915289

Print information available on the last page.

WestBow Press rev. date: 08/26/2022

Monday, April 30, 2018
1700 hours
Vance Air Force Base, Oklahoma Special Operations Training Division, US Air Force

Sergeant William Cutler had just sighted a funnel cloud approaching the air base tarmac. He sounded the tornado warning. Personnel scrambled for cover. Within ten minutes, the buildings were heavily damaged, and planes were tipped over. With only a few bumps and bruises, all two hundred personnel were fine.

Unfortunately, this was not the case for the small town of Shelbyville. It received heavy damage and ten deaths.

Sergeant Cutler had an idea, which he related to his commanding officer. "Someday, we will be able to stop those twisters with our military might. And just maybe we could be fortunate enough to succeed, so we can help mankind from these terrible storms."

His commanding officer replied, "I would love to see it in my lifetime."

***

Ten years later
Friday, August 18, 2028
0900 hours
Southridge Air Force Base, Anchorage, Alaska.

As several top-notch Air Force pilots gather in front of the commander's office, they are reading something on the bulletin board.

"Hey what's going on, dudes?" asks Josie Martin.

"Oh, sorry Josie. Just keep cool and read. Some people are so touchy."

The young pilots continue reading.

> Wanted: Pilots to be trained in a special operations program unit. We are seeking volunteers for this strategic training mission. Submit resume to

Commander William Cutler in care
of Vance Air Force Base, Oklahoma
for placement in this program.

As the pilots finish reading this special notice, they talk among themselves. They are excited about this new type of mission. Some prepare to send their resumes, while others are not interested.

"Hey guys, I heard fighter pilot Aidan Smith say that twenty-two pilots will try out for this special assignment. And that only six will be picked," says Josie.

"But hey, we have nothing to lose, right? We're all temporaries—just test pilots," exclaims Josie. "So good luck to all of you." She turns and heads back down the hallway to her barracks.

"I'm puzzled," says Richard Mackinder. "They did not give us much information on what we would be training for. They call it a *special mission*, hum.

"Yea, 'send in your resume.' I am in. I like a mystery," Richard continues. "Maybe it's a secret mission somewhere, someplace unknown."

After reading the information, they all ponder its meaning.

"Maybe we can solve this mystery. Let us ask the commander. Maybe he can shed some light on this," states Richard.

They disperse and continue with their duties.

***

After several weeks pass, Commander Stevens orders all fighter pilots to assemble in the ready room at 0900, Tuesday, October 10, 2028.

As pilots assemble, there is a buzz heard among them.

"What's up now?" asks Aidan Smith.

"What did you guys do now?" exclaims Josie.

"Ah, Josie, can it, and sit down. Save it for the captain," says Cole Davis.

"Attention!" Richard Mackinder states to everyone.

Sergeant Higbea enters the ready room. "Pilots, it has come to my attention that Vance Air Force Base in Oklahoma has chosen twelve of you for a special operations mission assignment. You twelve will be relocated to Vance within the next six months. Should you no longer want to fulfill your assignment, or if you change your mind, let me know this week so others can be chosen. I will say this: you pilots are the best I have ever known. If you were not chosen, do not be discouraged. Any questions?"

"Yes sir," replies Josie Martin. "Any idea how long this special training will be, and what is it for? Will all twelve pilots be transferred to Oklahoma?"

All twelve pilots will be sent to Oklahoma—only six will be chosen. You will all continue your training here until further notice. I cannot tell you much more at this time. Commander Cutler will fill you all in once you reach Vance. I know you will do your absolute best because you have demonstrated it to me. I am proud of you all. Those who were chosen, I will call you to my office personally. With that, you are dismissed."

* * *

Three weeks later
November 7, 2028

Commander Higbea gives notice to those who were chosen and instructs them to meet with him in the ready room. The six people are Josie Martin, David Jones, Mike Melbourne, Richard

Mackinder, Cole Davis, and Aidan Smith; one of them will be an alternate.

***

Three months later February 7, 2029

They arrive at Vance Air Force Base in Oklahoma. Pilots are assigned living quarters according to their and their family's needs. Singles will live in the barracks on base. Families will live in the base housing units and will stay there for the duration of the training.

Pilot	Personal Information	Military Status	Types of Aircraft	Missions
Josie Martin	Age 22-Single	Air Force Pilot 5 years	F-15 Eagle F-22 Raptor	Bombing Raids Afghanistan-Iraq
Aidan Smith	Age 27-Wife Kim-One Child	Air Force Pilot 9 years	F-35 Lightning 11	Bombing Raids Afghanistan-Iraq
Richard Mackinder	Age 28-Wife Teresa	Air Force Pilot 10 years	F-16 Fighting Falcon F-15 Eagle	Bombing Raids Iraq
David Jones	Age 24-Single	Air Force Pilot 5 years	F-15 Eagle	Convoy Protection Iraq

Mike Melbourne	Age 30- Wife Barb Two Children	Air Force Pilot 10 years	F-15 Eagle	Bombing Raids Iraq
Cole Davis	Age 25-Single	Air Force Pilot 7 years	F-22 Raptor F-16 Fighting Falcon	Bombing Targets Afghanistan

As the pilots and their families settle into their new homes, their moods turn somber the moment reality sets in.

The next morning, they discuss their feelings with each other. "One thing for certain about the Air Force," exclaims Richard, "they don't mess around." Josie asks the group, "You remember what we said in Alaska?"

"Remember, we're all a team," chimes in Cole.

"Yea, team for what?" asks David.

"Hey," Aidan says, "we must be good for something, after all, they picked us."

Mike shakes his head, "You are just letting your minds wander too much. Let us just settle in and take one day at a time."

At this time, the pilots continue with their daily assignments. They continue to wait for word on their special operation assignment.

***

November 20, 2029

The pilots receive notification they are to report to the ready room at 0800 to see Commander Cutler. As the pilots once again begin assembling, the mood seems to be excitement and mystery. Commander Cutler walks in, and they all stand at attention.

"At ease, and please be seated," the Commander says. "I will start out with why you are here, or why you were chosen for this mission. I can say this—your records speak for themselves. Each and every one of you has a special ability.

These abilities will enable us to succeed with this mission assignment.

"Now, over the next several months you will be trained to approach tornados. Yes, I said tornados! Today's technologies will enable us to accomplish this dangerous operation. I know what you are all thinking now, but before you start asking questions, hear me out. Then you can decide if you want to stay and continue with the training for this mission, or if you wish to pull out. I will tell you this has been in the works for ten years, and the Air Force feels it is time to act. Our mission is to approach a twister and drop what we call a *smart bomb* into the upper part of the vortex. That, in turn, will dissipate the twister once and for all.

"Now I know you have many questions, like for instance, why don't we just shoot a missile there and do the same thing? If you remember, or if you know anything about tornados, they include debris such as trees, cars, buildings—you name it. These can all be in the vortex. This would, in turn, affect the missile's point of entry. Therefore, the twister would not be disabled. This is why we will have five aircraft.

"You will have one lead aircraft equipped with the smart bomb, and four other aircraft that will protect the lead aircraft from debris. If you are worried about lightning striking the aircrafts in flight around the vortex, they have a special coating that resists electrical charges.

"The aircraft will be equipped with onboard radar systems that will detect any incoming debris and will activate the beam firing mechanism, which will destroy any type of debris around the twister. We have actually tested them on storms successfully.

"Go home and think it over. Talk it over with your families and let me know if you want to continue to accept this mission. Make your final decisions and report to me tomorrow at 0900 in the ready room. Dismissed!"

As the pilots returned to their living quarters, the only thing on their minds is how to explain this new mission to their family members.

Josie calls her mom and dad, excited about her new mission.

Her mother answers the telephone. She is excited to hear from Josie. "What's new?"

"I just wanted to touch base with you about why we were sent here to Oklahoma."

"Oh yea, why?" questions her mother.

"Because it's tornado alley," replies Josie.

"What do tornados have to do with you, daughter?"

"They have devised a way for our aircraft to approach a twister and fire a new bomb into the center to make it dissipate."

"You're not serious!"

"Yes, I am."

"How could you possibly make a tornado dissipate?"

"That's the theory of the US Air Force—that's all I can say."

"I will tell your father, but he will want to talk to you, so expect a call. Take care of yourself. We will talk later."

"Okay. Bye Mom."

When Richard arrives home to his wife Teresa and their children, right away she notices a strange look on her husband's face. "What is going on?" she asks.

Richard replies, "Remember the time when the twister went through Augusta?"

"What does a twister have to do with anything?"

"Our new mission is just that. We are to approach a twister as a team and drop what they call a smart bomb into the vortex, and hope it dissipates the funnel cloud. Tell me how you feel about this mission. I am still in disbelief.

"Well, personally I would rather fly into the vortex of a twister than into open airspace in Iraq where you're an easy target."

"Is this a top-secret mission?" asks Teresa.

"No, this is a mission that would help mankind a great deal, making it very worthwhile. I tell you this: we will pray about it and wait and see how it goes."

Cole returns to his quarters and calls his twin brother Brendan. He feels confident about the new mission; he thinks to himself, *this is right up my alley.*

His brother answers the telephone. "How is it going Ace? How is this secret mission that you spoke of last month?" Brendan asks.

"Now, it's not really a secret mission but what they told us really blew us out of the water," Cole tells him.

"Go on. I am listening."

"We are to approach a tornado and drop a special type of bomb inside that should dissipate the vortex."

"Okay, can this actually be done?"

"Only in theory."

"So, when do you start training for this so-called twister chasing mission?"

"The training starts tomorrow."

"I'll say this," remarks Brendan, the Air Force has chosen the best pilots possible."

"I agree with you: my friends are the best pilots," Cole tells Brendan. "There were twenty-two pilots picked, but only five of us made it this far. It makes me proud to be in the United States Air Force."

"Yes, and just think of the lives that could be saved should this type of innovative technology work. Best of luck to you and all your friends. Go Air Force! Talk to you later."

Mike meets his wife Barbara at the door. He gives his wife a hug and they walk to the living room.

How did it go today?" she asks.

"Surprisingly, good."

"So, can you now talk about your new secret mission or is it still a secret?"

"Remember when we watched the movie *Twister*? How were we taken in by its marvelous power and all that the twister does to terrify people by leveling small towns? How we, along with the children, watched it over and over again?"

"Okay, what does a twister have to do with your new mission?"

"Our new mission is to approach a twister, drop a special bomb inside, and kind of like blow it out."

"You're serious aren't you?"

"It is not a top-secret mission; the public will know as soon as we start approaching twisters. What do you think?"

"I think it would be fantastic if it could actually be done. Just think you could stop a twister before it destroys a town, and we are successful the entire world would benefit from such a maneuver. I agree."

"Now," Mike says, "I want the children to know how I feel. They are old enough to take in what I will tell them." Barbara agrees.

As David returns to his barracks, he thinks about his father, a retired Air Force corporal. Although they have not been on speaking terms for a couple of years, he decides to call home. His father answers the telephone.

"Hi Dad."

"Hi son," his father says, "it has been a while. I guess you have been busy training in the Air Force for whatever you're training for."

"Well, you know how that goes Dad. You have been in my shoes too. I have indeed been terribly busy in the Air Force. Day in and day out they train, train, train. It has kept me busy, and I have not had time to call you and Mom."

"That is understandable son. Your mother has informed me they have moved you to Vance Air Force Base."

"That's true Dad."

"She also mentioned something about a new mission; can you tell me what it is?"

"We are being trained to approach a tornado."

"Go on."

"There is a team of five of us. One will carry what they call a smart bomb, and the other four are protector type aircraft to protect from debris. And, in theory, the Air Force believes that this will terminate a twister."

"That sounds exciting. I wish I were there. I hope it works, son. That would save a lot of lives and a lot of damage. Tell all your squad members, I wish them the best of luck. Talk to you soon."

Aidan enters his barracks and the first thing he thinks of is his kid sister, Davia. He picks up his cell and gives her a call.

She answers the phone and says, "Hey Aidan, I know you have been busy, but can you still call once in a while?"

"Yea, but sometimes you're a hard one to reach," says Aidan.

"Mom says you have been transferred to Vance Air Force Base, Oklahoma. Why?"

"I volunteered to come here for a special operations mission."

"Can you elaborate on what you will be doing?"

"I can, but it sounds like science fiction."

"So, tell me."

"It seems the Air Force has developed a new type of weapon. We are to approach a tornado and use this device to snuff a twister or tornado out."

"You're right—it does sound like science fiction, but if it works it would be a great blessing from God."

"Well, you know I put my trust in God to keep us safe, and if this can be done it will be only through His will."

"Should I tell Mother and Dad?"

"I wish you would because you know how they will feel about it."

"Okay, consider it done. I love you. Goodbye for now."

When the pilots return the next day at 0900 hours, they once again stand at attention when Commander Cutler enters the room.

"Relax, pilots, and be seated. Now I need to know how many of you plan to stay the course for this mission or opting out now."

All the pilots reply, "Stay the course!"

"Thank you, pilots. That takes a lot off my mind. Consider this your first day of training.

"You have noticed the flight simulators that are presently in the training room. These simulators are comparable to the aircraft you will be assigned to for this mission. You will be trained in these simulators to help you see and feel what it is like to be next to an actual twister. And believe me, you will be glad you did. The dangerous wind currents, down drafts, lightning, thick dust, and dirt will all be simulated just exactly like the cockpit.

"Due to the fact that all these perils will affect your vision, you will learn how to react to the different scenarios during this time. You will be trained on your guidance system radar, weapon system, and computer systems. The computer will automatically lock in the target of the lead plane. The weapon can be fired by the lead pilot once the sequence is complete.

"Now I know most of you have some knowledge of tornados and natural disasters, but believe me, we do not know it all. For the next three days, you will be trained in these simulators. So, after you take a lunch break, please return here to begin training. Just one more thing I need from you five: you need to pick a squad leader. I am sure you can come to some conclusion by yourselves. If not, I will pick. Dismissed."

As the group approaches the mess hall, they discuss who should be the squad leader.

"I already know who the leader should be," says Josie.

"Yes, who?" inquire the other pilots.

"Richard should be."

"Me?" says Richard. "Are you sure you want me as your squad leader?"

They all reply, "Yes, sir."

As they return to the ready room to begin their simulator training, David says, "Those simulators are pretty cool."

Cole replies, "Yea, I only crashed twice in the ones used for our original training. But I tell you this they sure instruct pilots how to fly."

As Commander Cutler returns to the ready room, Sergeant Armor follows right behind.

Commander Cutler tells the pilots just to relax. "You all know Sergeant Armor; he will now be your instructor for the final leg of your training mission. Our mission is called 'Tornado Intercept.' After your simulator training, Sergeant Armor will instruct you on your flight formation to approach the tornado. You will only approach twisters as they move away from us. This will allow for us have time for evasive maneuvers in emergency situations.

"One more item Sergeant Armor will explain to you pilots, should there be any problems with the aircraft: abort and return to base. For any reason, if you lose two aircraft due to mechanical issues, the remaining three can continue to conduct the mission. This is providing the lead aircraft is still present. You all know the Air Force Code: 'no pilot flies alone.' So, remember these rules. Pilots, here is Sergeant Armor."

"Now before we start simulators, we will watch a short film on tornados. This film is a military film, and you will see three jets approaching an F-5 twister. The computer system of the aircraft recorded all movements, debris, etc. that are programed in your simulators. That is why this training is so important. This film will also show you things we never knew a twister could do, so pay careful attention."

As the film begins, the pilots realize just how dangerous an F-4 or F-5 can be. They see a twister pick up a train engine, boxcars, and trees. They also see how far up the vortex debris can be carried, not to mention the thick dust and dirt along with lightning. They realize just how important this mission is.

As the film ends, Sergeant Armor explains, "You will not deploy for smaller tornados because they dissipate too rapidly. And with that, you are dismissed."

The following day the pilots return to the ready room at 0800 hours. As they enter the room, Sergeant Armor is already there and greets them with "Good morning, and please be seated." Sergeant Armor explains to the pilots, "These simulators that you will be training on are designed and equipped just the same as the jet aircraft that you will be flying. Our intension is to show you exactly how it feels to be next to a twister. We are not going to retrain you as pilots—you are already the best at what you do, and I would like to thank each one of you."

As each pilot enters a simulator, the pilot begins to make the aircraft ready for take-off. Sergeant Armor explains to them they will be taught to fly in a new formation as they approach the twister. Therefore, simulators will instruct each plane to its flight location and then move it into formation.

"Once this is accomplished," continues Sergeant Armor, "the team will approach the twister. The computer will then instruct you about your air speed and your flight formation. It will also activate the radar and weapons systems. The computer will also instruct the lead aircraft to its correct position. The pilot of the lead aircraft will arm weapons and the computer will detect where smart bombs will be launched into the vortex.

"These simulators will replicate air currents, downdrafts, updrafts, and things that you do not usually feel during normal maneuvers. Once the weapon system has been activated, lasers are online. This should all occur when you are in formation to launch the smart bomb into vortex. These lasers will automatically destroy any incoming objects. Your lasers are not designed to destroy objects on the ground.

"Pilots, as you watched in the military training film, you saw objects as large as a train engine being picked up. They do not travel up the vortex far before they are dropped. Items such as boats, small trees, roofs, highway signs, etc. will be easily destroyed by the laser. Good luck pilots. Your simulation starts. Do what you do best."

As the pilots complete their tasks and one by one return to base, they await word from the simulator computer to see if the mission was accomplished. As they wait, they talk with each other, and all agree the task was not easy. They were all happy to have had this type of simulation practice since it was indeed complicated.

The pilots do not have to wait long as Sergeant Armor enters the training room. "Pilots, I have your test scores and I will tell you that as a team your need at least a 96 percent or better to pass. Congratulations! You scored 97 percent. Wonderful job. This means you have completed your training with the simulators."

They all cheer.

"What's next?" asks Josie.

"You will all meet me Monday morning on the tarmac at Hangar 5. There you will train several days in this type of formation, until you all feel comfortable with this new type of aircraft, the

F-22 Raptors. I will see you first thing Monday morning at 0800 hours. Make sure you get a good weekend's rest. Dismissed."

Once they dismiss, they all talk to one another about the training.

Cole says, "It really shakes you up in the twister. I am glad we did this simulation training. It will give me more confidence."

They all agree.

"I'll tell you this," says Richard, "I will be happy when we have one behind us. That would give me confidence."

"Enjoy your weekend, gang," Josie says.

On Monday at 0800 hours, the pilots arrive at Hangar 5 on the tarmac. Commander Cutler and Sergeant Armor are already there. When the pilots see the brand-new aircraft lined up on the tarmac, they all get caught up in amazement at what they see.

"Wow!" exclaims Josie.

"That's what I said when they arrived," responds Commander Cutler.

Sergeant Armor explains to the pilots, "It doesn't matter which plane you like, so climb aboard and make ready your aircraft for take-off once you have permission from the tower."

Commander Cutler tells them, "Go do what you do best, learn your formation, and return to base. You could also practice your twister approach as if there is a real twister in front of you. Return to base and report to me any problems you have with the new aircraft. I will tell you this, you are already on stand-by alert and will be deployed should the need occur to approach a real twister."

As the pilots take off one-by-one, they climb to 5,000 feet. They perform a computer analysis: everything from launching the smart bomb to radar and weapons check. They always maintain their formation. The pilots are all excited about how the aircraft handle and all systems function normally. They return to base. They report their findings to Commander Cutler and Sergeant Armor.

Sergeant Armor tells the pilots they will now continue their daily routines as pilots with their duties on base, maintaining their aircraft until they go on alert for an actual tornado mission run. "You are dismissed to your normal activities. Any problems or questions, please see me."

April 28, 2030, as normal springtime weather conditions prevail, the pilots continue their daily activities. Those activities will change dramatically the next day.

On April 29 at 1000 hours, the emergency alert system on the radio announces that the National Weather Service issued a tornado watch effective immediately in Oklahoma for the following areas: the southern part of Oklahoma City as well as Vance Air Force Base, and the city of Enid, Oklahoma until 6 p.m. These storms will produce damaging winds, hail, and possible tornados. Please pay attention to the changing weather conditions as these storms are developing rapidly.

As the pilots are notified that they are on alert, they must prep their F-22 Raptor aircraft for immediate departure. At 1400 hours, the pilots receive word that a possible F-4 or F-5 has formed. The pilots receive permission to enter their craft and prepare for take-off. At 1430 hours, the pilots take off from Vance Air Force Base. As the pilots ascend to their altitude of 4,500 feet, they assume their formation pattern.

They are seventy miles out from the twister.

"Squad leader to the team," says Richard. "Can everyone hear me?"

They all answer yes.

Sixty miles out from the Air Force base, Josie tells the squad leader she is having computer systems problems with the aircraft.

"You'll have to return to base Josie," replies the squad leader, "and I will need a volunteer to follow her. Sorry."

David replies, "I'll go with her."

"Roger that," says the squad leader as the two jets veer away from the formation and head back.

"Assume the same type of formation," Richard says to Mike and Aidan.

"Roger that," they reply.

"We can still pull this mission off with just three of us; remember what Commander Cutler told us." The other pilots agree.

The aircraft make their descent to 1,000 feet just below the storm wall. As the computer brings the aircraft parallel with the funnel cloud, they finally get a good look at this huge tornado. They all look in awe at the destruction below.

"I know guys, we want to look at this thing, but that is not what we are here for. Let us make ready and do the job we were trained to do," says Richard.

As the aircraft enter the turbulence of the twister, they realize how dangerous this assignment is. Lasers begin shooting debris heading toward the aircraft. Lightning is also a factor. The leader aircraft locks in the target for bomb launch into the precise location of the vortex and the computer verifies the location.

"I will give a signal to Richard when to push the launch button," says Aidan. At 1500 hours, the smart bomb is launched into the vortex and all three aircraft ascend to a higher altitude to escape harm's way.

Richard radios Mike and Aidan and explains, "We will have to wait for word from the base tower to see if mission is complete or if we need to resume attack."

As the pilots fly around, the National Weather Service in Oklahoma reports to the base commander that they recorded a detonation at approximately 1501 hours and the funnel dissipated at 1504 hours.

As word gets back to the pilots, they are all extremely happy.

Richard says, "I guess the brick wall theory worked with the smart bomb."

Mike says, "Hallelujah."

Aidan replies, "Praise the Lord."

As all the good news comes back to the pilots, Richard asks the base tower, "I need to know about my two pilots I sent back, Josie and David."

The base tower answers, "They are here, safe and sound. You may return to base."

As the planes land safely back at Vance Air Force Base, they return to a hero's welcome; with Josie, David, Commander Cutler, and Sergeant Armor leading the way.

Thank you too all that have served our Country in the Military including my friends and family.

Glenn Cutler, Army

Roger Wedig, Army

Ron Armour, Army

Norman Lawson, Army

William Cutler, Army

Mark Cutler, USAF

Ralph McKendrick, Army

Larry Welton, Army

Carl Osterling, Army

Joe Fields, Army

Ed Higbee, USAF

David Bradshaw, Marines

And many more

Printed in the United States
by Baker & Taylor Publisher Services